Fancy NANCY

Bonjour, Butterfly

Written by
Jane O'Connor

Illustrated by
Robin Preiss Glasser

HarperCollinsPublishers

For my favorite butterfly breeders—
Robby and Teddy—with love
—J. O'C.

For Edith Pick Lindner—for me, the
model of beauty and elegance
—R.P.G.

Fancy Nancy: Bonjour, Butterfly
Text copyright © 2008 by Jane O'Connor
Illustrations copyright © 2008 by Robin Preiss Glasser
Printed in the U.S.A.
For information address HarperCollins Children's Books, a division of HarperCollins Publishers,
1350 Avenue of the Americas, New York, NY 10019.
www.harpercollinschildrens.com
Library of Congress Cataloging-in-Publication Data
O'Connor, Jane.
    Bonjour, butterfly / written by Jane O'Connor ; illustrated by Robin Preiss Glasser. — 1st ed.
        p.   cm. — (Fancy Nancy)
    Summary: Nancy is furious when she cannot go to her friend Bree's butterfly-themed birthday party, but her family's
outing might just be extraordinary enough to make her feel better.
    ISBN 978-0-06-123588-7 (trade bdg.)
    ISBN 978-0-06-123589-4 (lib. bdg.)
    [1. Butterflies—Fiction. 2. Parties—Fiction. 3. Birthdays—Fiction. 4. Grandparents—Fiction. 5. Anniversaries—
Fiction.] I. Preiss-Glasser, Robin, ill. II. Title.
PZ7.O222Bon 2008   2007030696
[E]—dc22   CIP
                                                                                                                                AC
Typography by Jeanne L. Hogle
3 4 5 6 7 8 9 10
❖
First Edition

$\mathcal{D}$on't you think butterflies are exquisite?
(Exquisite is even fancier than beautiful.)

Whenever my friend Bree and I see one, we say, "Bonjour!" That's French for "hello!"

"Do butterflies understand French?" my dad asks.
"Maybe," I tell him.

Bree's birthday party is soon. Everything will look like butterflies—even the cake.

I show her how to turn the Bs into butterflies——on the invitations.

"You're so lucky your name begins with a B," I tell her.

&Bree's
&Butterfly
&Birthday
Saturday at noon

Come as your favorite &Butterfly

R.S.V.P.

R.S.V.P. is short for *Répondez s'il vous plaît.*
That's French for please reply.

I'm going as an azure butterfly.
My wings are bright blue and—what's that fancy
word for shiny? Oh, yes! Iridescent.

"Bree's party is this Saturday! I can't wait!"
"Oh no!" cries my mom. "I totally forgot."

Then she says I can't go! My grandparents' anniversary party is the same day.

Mom says, "Bree's birthday is special. But being married for fifty years—that's exceptional. That's extraordinary!"

If my mother thinks using fancy words will make me feel better, she's wrong!

When I tell Bree I can't come, she is heartbroken.

For the next two days,
I scowl

and sulk

and storm around the house.

Mad is way too plain for how I feel.

I am furious!

On the train, the only person I talk to is
Marabelle. We mostly speak in French.

I perk up a little at the station.
My grandparents are so thrilled to see me.

Grandpa says, "It wouldn't be a party without our glamorous granddaughter."

I must say, the City Squire Motel is quite elegant.
(That's a fancy word for fancy.) I curtsy to everyone.

There is a candy machine in the hall
and an automatic ice dispenser.

In the bathroom are little bottles of bath gel and shampoo and cream.

Ooh la la! It's like being at a beauty spa.

At the party, I have so much fun,
I forget to be furious.

Grandpa teaches me the cha-cha.

Waiters bring out tiny hot dogs
on silver platters.
    "Mmm. Delicious,
darling," I tell my sister.
"You must try one."

Later I whisper, "I'm sorry
for the way I behaved. I am
ecstatic to be here."

It really is an extraordinary night.

The next morning, my mother wakes me up. "Grandma says the zoo here has a butterfly garden. Do you want to go?"

"Oui, oui, oui!" That's French for "yes, yes, yes!"

My grandparents meet us at the zoo. "Those are monarch butterflies on your tie," I tell Grandpa.

"My! You know a lot about butterflies," he says.
"Yes," I admit. "I am practically an expert."

The butterfly garden is gorgeous.
(Gorgeous is also fancier than beautiful.)
I can't wait to tell Bree about it.

Suddenly a little blue butterfly flits toward me—
an azure butterfly.
   All butterflies are special, but this one is extraordinary.
"Bonjour," I say.

You know what?

I am nearly positive butterflies understand French.